Dear Parent:

Congratulations! Your child is taking the first steps on an exciting journey. The destination? Independent reading!

STEP INTO READING® will help your child get there. The program offers books at five levels that accompany children from their first attempts at reading to reading success. Each step includes fun stories, fiction and nonfiction, and colorful art. There are also Step into Reading Sticker Books, Step into Reading Math Readers, Step into Reading Write-In Readers, Step into Reading Phonics Readers, and Step into Reading Phonics First Steps! Boxed Sets—a complete literacy program with something to interest every child.

Learning to Read, Step by Step!

Ready to Read Preschool–Kindergarten
• big type and easy words • rhyme and rhythm • picture clues
For children who know the alphabet and are eager to begin reading.

Reading with Help Preschool–Grade 1
• basic vocabulary • short sentences • simple stories
For children who recognize familiar words and sound out new words with help.

Reading on Your Own Grades 1–3
• engaging characters • easy-to-follow plots • popular topics
For children who are ready to read on their own.

Reading Paragraphs Grades 2–3
• challenging vocabulary • short paragraphs • exciting stories
For newly independent readers who read simple sentences with confidence.

Ready for Chapters Grades 2–4
• chapters • longer paragraphs • full-color art
For children who want to take the plunge into chapter books but still like colorful pictures.

STEP INTO READING® is designed to give every child a successful reading experience. The grade levels are only guides. Children can progress through the steps at their own speed, developing confidence in their reading, no matter what their grade.

Remember, a lifetime love of reading starts with a single step!

Step into Reading, Random House, and the Random House colophon are registered trademarks of Random House, Inc.

Visit us on the Web!
www.stepintoreading.com
www.randomhouse.com/kids/disney

Educators and librarians, for a variety of teaching tools, visit us at
www.randomhouse.com/teachers

ISBN: 978-0-7364-2554-4

Printed in the United States of America   20 19 18 17   First Edition

STEP INTO READING®

Featuring characters
from your favorite
Disney·PIXAR
movies!

Disney·PIXAR
Story Collection

Step 1 and Step 2 Books

A Collection of Five Early Readers

Random House 🏠 New York

Contents

DISNEY · PIXAR
RATATOUILLE
(rat·a·too·ee)

Run, Remy, Run!

By Kitty Richards

Illustrated by the Disney Storybook Artists

Random House 🏠 New York

This is Remy.

Remy is not like
the other rats.

He walks on two feet.

He reads books.

He watches TV.

He wants to be a chef!

One day, Remy gets lost.

He ends up in Paris.

Remy watches a boy
make soup.

The boy spills the soup.

What will he do?

The boy makes more soup.
But the soup is bad!

The skylight opens!

Remy falls down!

Remy lands in the sink.
Swim, Remy, swim!

Remy gets out.
But he is scared.

The kitchen is busy.
Run, Remy, run!

Remy sees

an open window.

Will he get out?

Climb, Remy, climb!

Oh, no!

Remy falls into a pot.

Jump, Remy, jump!

He lands in a pan!

Jump, Remy, jump!

Remy sees the boy.

The boy tastes the soup.
Yuck!

Run, Remy, run!

But Remy stops running.

He smells the soup.

The soup stinks!

Remy wants to fix it.

Cook, Remy, cook!

Uh-oh!

The boy sees Remy.

The chef sees the boy.

He is angry.

No one is watching.

The soup gets served!

Will the soup
taste good?

Yes!

That rat can cook!

DISNEY · PIXAR

FINDING NEMO

Just Keep Swimming

By Melissa Lagonegro

Illustrated by Atelier Philippe Harchy

Random House 🏠 New York

Nemo has a dream.
He wants to join
the school swim team.

But Nemo has
a little fin.

He thinks that
he will never win.

Dory helps Nemo.

She teaches him
to go, go, go!

Nemo races and races.

Nemo chases and chases.

"Just keep swimming,"
Dory sings.

But Nemo thinks
of other things.

"I will never win.
I have a bad fin."

"Just keep swimming!"
Dory cries.

So Nemo tries . . .

and tries . . .

. . . and tries.

Nemo races and races.

Nemo chases and chases.

Yippee! Yahoo!

His dream comes true.

Nemo makes the team.

Can Nemo win the
first-place prize?

"Just keep swimming!"
Dory cries.

Watch him race.

Watch him chase.

Watch as Nemo wins
first place!

Disney · PIXAR
THE WORLD OF

Cars

Driving Buddies

Adapted by Apple Jordan

Illustrated by the Disney Storybook Artists

Inspired by the art and character designs created by Pixar Animation Studios

Random House 🏠 New York

McQueen was

a race car.

He was shiny and fast.

He wanted one thing—
to win the big race!

Mater was a tow truck.
He was old and rusty.
He wanted one thing—
a best friend.

Mater lived
in a little town.
The streets were quiet.
All was calm.

One night,
McQueen got lost
on his way
to the big race.

He sped into
the little town.
Sheriff chased him.
McQueen got scared!

He flew into fences!

He crashed into cones!

He ripped up the road!

He made a big mess.

McQueen was
sent to jail.
He met Mater there.
Mater liked
McQueen right away.

Sally, the town lawyer,
and the other cars
wanted McQueen
to fix the road.

McQueen could not
leave town until
the job was done.

McQueen got to work.

He was unhappy.

Mater wanted

to show him some fun.

He took McQueen
tractor tipping.
It <u>was</u> fun.

McQueen told Mater
why he wanted
to win the big race.

He would have fame
and a new look.
He would be a winner!

Mater was happy.
He had
a new best friend.

McQueen fixed
the road at last!
The news reporters
found McQueen!

Mack the truck
was glad to see him!
It was time to go
to the big race.

Mater was sad
to see his buddy leave.
The other cars
were sad, too.

So Mater and his friends
went to the racetrack.
They helped McQueen.

But McQueen still
did not win.
He helped an old friend
finish the race instead.

Now he knew
that winning was not
what he wanted most.

What he wanted most
were friends.

DISNEY · PIXAR

TOY STORY AND BEYOND!

Buzz's Backpack Adventure

By Apple Jordan
Illustrated by Alex Maher

Random House 🏠 New York

Andy could not
wait for school.
Today was
space day!

"I will bring
my space ranger,
Buzz Lightyear,"
he said.

Buzz was excited.

He loved

space day!

In class, Andy
learned
about space.

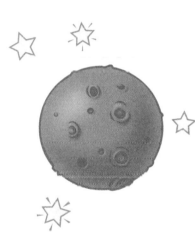 He learned
about the stars
and the moon.

He learned
about the sun
and the planets.

Brring!

The bell rang.

Lunchtime!

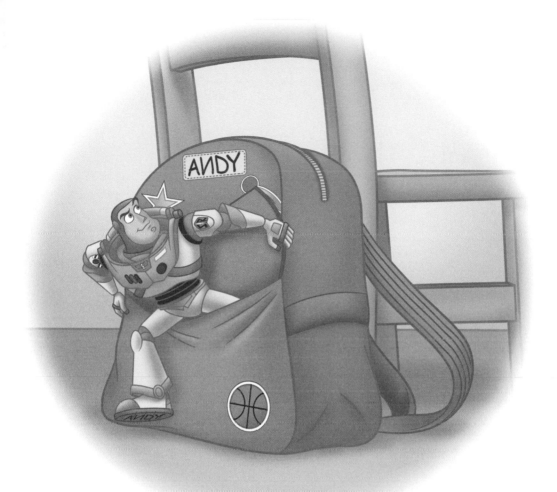

Buzz hopped out
of Andy's backpack.
He was ready
for fun!

Buzz saw the stars
and the moon.

He saw the planets.

Buzz could not
wait to explore.

Buzz saw
a hamster.
"Greetings,
strange creature,"
he said.

Buzz lifted the lid
to get a closer look.

Uh-oh!
The hamster
jumped out.
It ran off.

"Come back!"

Buzz cried.

"I mean you no harm."

Oops!
Buzz fell into
a jar of paint.

"Blast!" cried Buzz.
"I must clean
up and find
that creature."

Buzz looked for

the hamster

inside a desk.

Buzz saw old gum
and chewed pencils,
but no hamster.

Then Buzz met
some clay aliens.
He thought they
were space toys.

"Greetings,"
he said.
"Have you seen a
furry creature?"

They did not
answer.
Buzz shook hands
with a space toy.
Its arm fell off.

"Sorry about that!"
Buzz cried.

He ran away.

Buzz landed on
a tower made
of blocks.

It wobbled
back and forth.
Crash!
At last it came
toppling down.

"Oh, no!" said Buzz. "I must clean up this big mess!"

"All done!" said Buzz.
Then the bell rang.
The class came
back from lunch.

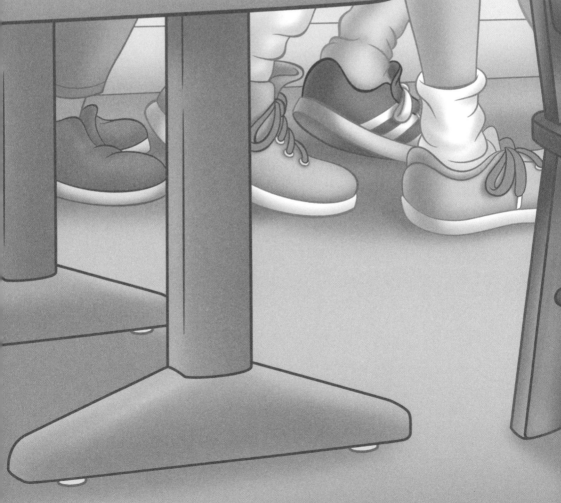

Buzz hopped
into Andy's backpack.
No one saw him.

The class got ready
for show-and-tell.
Andy went first.

"This is Buzz,"
he said.
"Buzz is the BEST
space ranger ever!"

DISNEY·PIXAR
MONSTERS, INC.
Boo on the Loose

Illustrated by Scott Tilley,
Floyd Norman, and Brooks Campbell

Random House 🏠 New York

Sulley was the top
Scarer at Monsters, Inc.
Scaring kids was
a big job!
Their screams kept
the city running.

Sulley worked
on the Scare Floor.
The red light meant
he could open the door.

Then Sulley could scare
the kid in the room!

Sulley was heading home at the end of his shift. He saw a door.

But all the doors
should have been put away.
"Is anybody there?" he asked.

"Boo!" something said.

It was a little girl!

"Aaaah!"

Sulley screamed.

Monsters thought
kids were unsafe.
Sulley tried
to get rid of her.
But nothing worked.

Sulley needed help.

He took the kid home.

"Her name is Boo,"

said Sulley.

"She cannot stay here!"
cried Mike.

He came up with a plan.

Sulley and Mike put Boo
in a monster suit.
They drove to the park
to leave her there.

But Boo locked herself
in the car!
"Get her out!"
yelled Mike.

But nothing worked.

Boo waved

from inside the car.

"What do we do now?"

Mike shouted.

A butterfly flew by.
Boo opened the door
and ran after it!

Mike grabbed Sulley.

"Let's go!"

shouted Mike.

Mike got in the car.

It would not start.

"We are out of gas!"

said Mike.

But Sulley was thinking
about Boo.

He missed her already.

Sulley had an idea!
"We need to find Boo!"
Sulley said.
"Her scream
will start the car."

Sulley ran
into the woods.
He called for Boo.

"Boo, where are you?"

he called.

Sulley found her.
Boo ran right to him.

Sulley walked
back to the car.
"You're holding
its hand!"
Mike cried.

Sulley smiled.
"And I feel fine!"
he said.

Sulley helped Boo
into the car.
"Now we need a scream,"
said Mike.

"You are the best Scarer
at Monsters, Inc.
Do your stuff!"
said Mike.

Boo smiled at Sulley.

Sulley could not roar.

He could not scare Boo!

"Scare it!" yelled Mike.

He banged his head.

The horn honked!

"Ouch!"

cried Mike.

Boo laughed.

The engine started!

Mike and Sulley

looked at each other.

How did <u>that</u> happen?

Mike looked at Boo.
"She can stay for now,"
he said.